This book is dedicated to a beautiful little girl
called Lola. Lola was a courageous, strong
willed and kind hearted girl who sadly lost her
battle with brain cancer in April, 2021.
She loved the ocean, swimming and
most of all, mermaids. Her one wish was
to become one. Lola's mum Penny believes
she would be tickled pink to know that
a main character in a book is named after her.
Penny hopes that anyone reading this
will be inspired to be brave, just like Lola.

Copyright © Majestic Whale Encounters
Authors: Sarah Cullen & Carmen Ellis
Artwork & Book Design © Zuzana Svobodová

Title: Lola, The Bracelet of Courage

ISBN 978-0-6453650-1-6 (Paperback)
ISBN 978-0-6453650-0-9 (Hardcover)
ISBN 978-0-6453650-2-3 (eBook)

LOLA

the
BRACELET
of COURAGE

written by
Sarah Cullen
Carmen Ellis

illustrated by
Zuzana
Svobodová

Lola the mermaid
seemed very courageous.
Some things that she did
were just simply outrageous!

She liked to tell stories of ghosts in the dark
and to go on fast rides at the fun water park.

But being this brave was not always the case.
She used to be timid and felt out of place.

Her dad said one day, "Please come here, Lola dear!
I've got something special to help with your fear.
This bracelet of courage with seashells and gold
has magical powers to make you feel bold."

When wearing the bracelet, she felt brave and strong
and no longer thought that she didn't belong.

One day, Lola went on a trip with her friends
to the waterfall pools where the valley transcends.

Of course, she would recklessly swing off the rope.
She'd climb up the rocks, and then slip down the slope.

Then suddenly Lola yelled out,
"It's not here! My bracelet
of courage is gone! Dear, oh, dear!"

She searched high and low, but gave up in despair,
then shockingly noticed her friends were not there.

The current had also just started to turn.

It's running too fast, Lola thought with concern.

"I'm so scared." Lola sighed, "But I have to go back.

Which way should I go? I must find a new track!"

"It's as if all my strength has at once disappeared!"
Going home on her own was what Lola had feared.
"Why are you sad?" asked a voice from behind.
She turned around quickly and what did she find?

She saw a grey dolphin with big friendly eyes
and told him the tale of her bracelet's demise.
"I need to get home, and you seem really nice."
The dolphin just smiled before giving advice.

"Your breathing can help keep you calm without doubt.
Take one deep breath in and then slowly breathe out.
If you want to find strength, I will give you a clue:
The COURAGE you seek, you will find it IN YOU."

The path through the forest
looked creepy and scary,
with kelp hanging down,
very slimy and hairy.

How she wished she could stop
and just call it a day.
But the comfort of home
was still ages away.

She closed her eyes shut and then entered at last.

The kelp touched her skin, and her heart raced so fast.

She opened her eyes once she'd counted to three.

There were sea urchins down on the floor of the sea.

The urchins all smiled and then gave her a cheer.

They sang her a song about conquering fear.

"If you want to find strength, we will give you a clue:

The COURAGE you seek, you will find it IN YOU."

She swam to the mouth of a jellyfish cave
and then said to herself. "You can do it! Be brave!"
With one big deep breath, she then popped her head through
and discovered a magical world in the blue,

where jellyfish sparkled in colors so bright.
They lit up the cave that was dark as the night.
Before going further, she stopped to think twice.
Then the jellyfish noticed and gave her advice.

"Think happy thoughts while you close your eyes tight.
Try to summon your courage with all of your might.
If you want to find strength, we will give you a clue:
The COURAGE you seek, you will find it IN YOU."

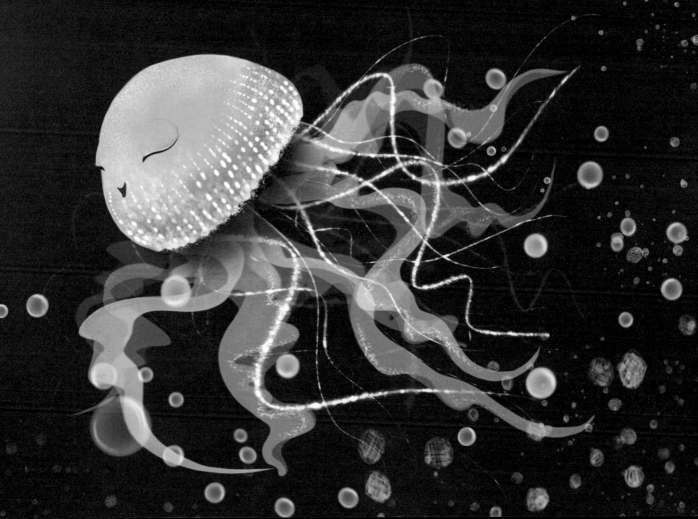

She was careful and wary, made sure not to touch,
but this cave she had feared, she now loved it so much!
She followed a brightly lit path homeward bound
that led her right back to her house, safe and sound.

Losing her bracelet had helped her to see
that no magical powers had set her strength free.
She had proven at last she was brave, she was strong.

"The COURAGE has been
IN MY HEART all along!"

Fun facts

1. If a mermaid is female, what is a male mermaid called?

A -Merchap

B -Merbloke

C -Merman

2. The first part of the word mermaid comes from the Old English word mere, meaning what?

A -Fish

B -Sea

C -Fin

3. Sea Urchins don't have eyes, so how do they see?

A -With their mouth

B -With their feet

C -With their nose

4. Scientists discovered a jellyfish that is believed to live forever, what is the name of that jellyfish?

A -Immortal jellyfish

B -Livelong jellyfish

C -Ifeelsoold jellyfish

5. What is kelp?

A -Animal

B -Algae

C -Plant

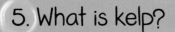

Answers

1. C (Merman)
2. B (Sea)
3. B (With their feet)
4. A (Immortal jellyfish)
5. B (Algae)

Hi there, Carmen and Sarah here. We are sisters from NSW, Australia. Together, we share a love of the ocean and all the beautiful creatures in it. Through these books, we would love to encourage children from all over the world to share their *passion of the ocean* and protect it for years to come. We welcome you to join us on Instagram and Facebook where you can see sneak peaks of future projects, learn more about the ocean and even help to choose names of characters and other decisions in the book making process.

These books would not be possible without our beautiful illustrator Zuzana Svobodová. If you want to follow Zuzana and see more of her *stunning illustrations*, her Instagram is @zuzana_svobodova_illustration.

We cannot thank you enough for your support. Without you we would not be able to keep making our beloved Ocean Tales. If you would like to help keep our dream alive, an honest review on Amazon would help us to spread the word.

Much love from our families to yours.

www.instagram.com/oceantaleschildrensbooks   www.facebook.com/Ocean-Tales-Childrens-Books-100332601636543   www.oceantaleschildrensbooks.com.au

Made in United States
North Haven, CT
16 January 2023